Boo Hoo Boo-Boo

by Marilyn Singer

illustrated by Elivia Savadier

HarperFestival®
A Division of HarperCollins*Publishers*

Look at Lulu,
Twirling in her tutu.

Shoe shoe, jump!

Shoe shoe, thump!

Oh, no! Boo hoo!
Lulu's got a boo-boo.

There goes Andrew,
Acting like a choo choo.

Whoo whoo, dash!

Whoo whoo, crash!

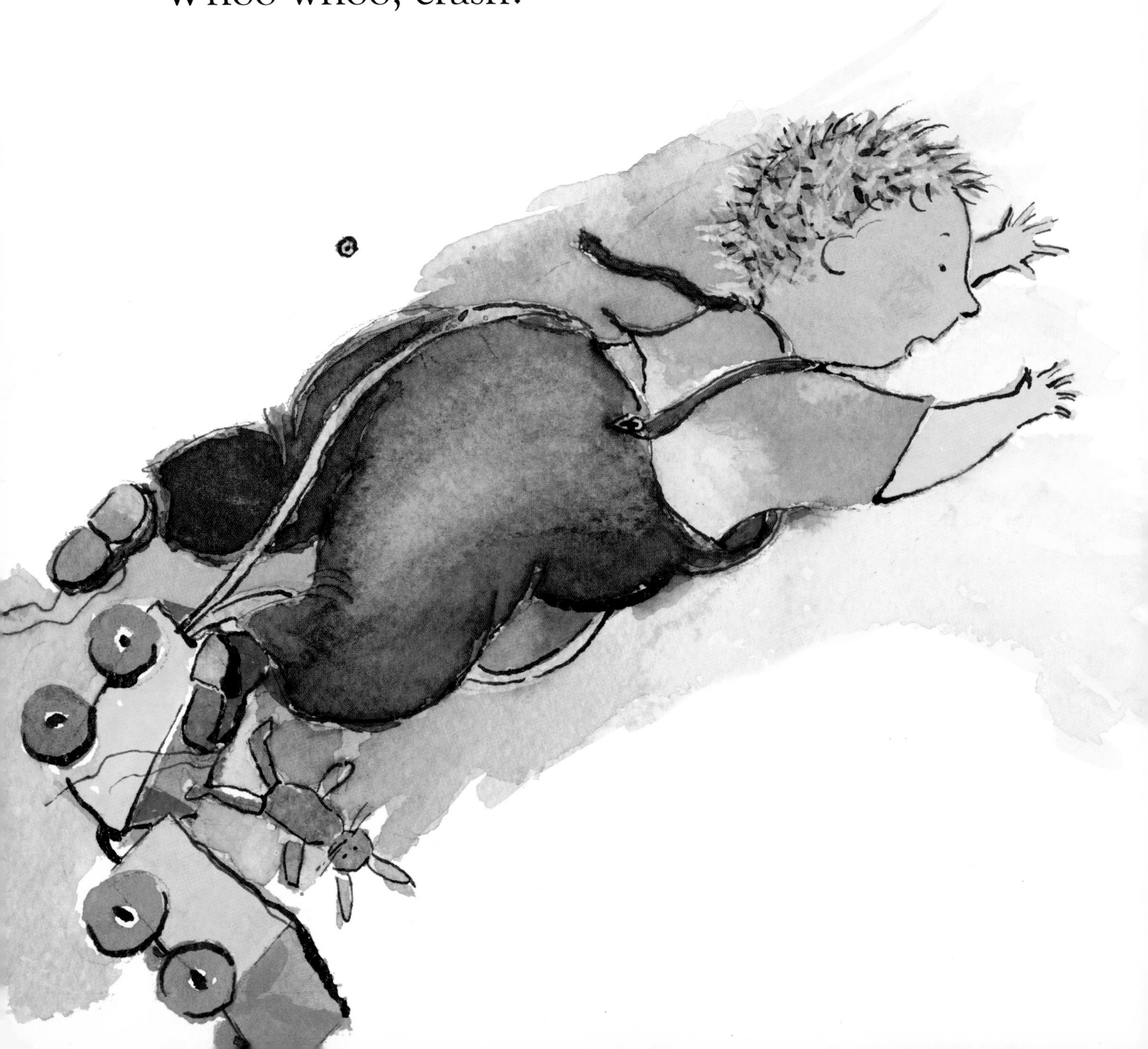

Oh, no! Boo hoo!
Andrew's got a boo-boo.

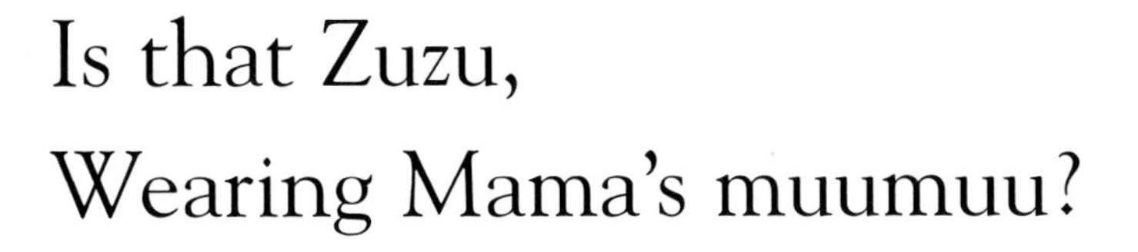

Is that Zuzu,
Wearing Mama's muumuu?

Ooh ooh, skip!

Ooh ooh, trip!

Oh, no! Boo hoo!
Zuzu's got a boo-boo.

Bad, bad boo-boo
Makes them want to boo hoo.
Bah bah, scowl!
Wah wah, howl!
Everyone feels blue.
Then what do they do?

Look at Lulu
Wash that nasty boo-boo.
There goes Andrew,
Smoothing soothing goo goo.
Is that Zuzu?
Bandage to the rescue!

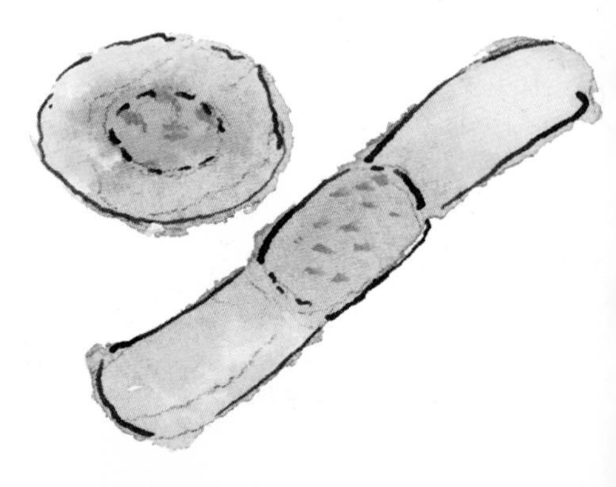

On their elbows,
On their knees,
They'll get three kisses,
Then a squeeze.

And in just a day or two,